For Carrie
—Jarrett

For Marcela
—Jerome

Cover design by Aram Kim.

Copyright © 2020 by Jarrett Pumphrey and Jerome Pumphrey.
All rights reserved. Published by Scholastic Inc., 557 Broadway, New York, NY 10012,
by arrangement with W. W. Norton & Company, Inc.
Printed in the U.S.A.

ISBN-13: 978-1-338-78195-3
ISBN-10: 1-338-78195-2

2 3 4 5 6 7 8 9 10   40   30 29 28 27 26 25 24 23 22 21

Scholastic Inc., 557 Broadway, New York, NY 10012

Jarrett Pumphrey   Jerome Pumphrey

THE OLD TRUCK

SCHOLASTIC INC.

On a small farm, an old truck worked hard.

The old truck worked long.

The old truck grew weary and tired.

So the old truck rested

and dreamed.

The old truck sailed the seas,

braved the skies,

and chased the stars.

But the old truck grew older.

And older.

And older still.

On a small farm, a new farmer worked hard.

The new farmer worked long.

The new farmer grew weary and tired.

But she dreamed

and persisted.

VROOOOOOOM!!

On a small farm, an old truck worked hard.

Jarrett and **Jerome Pumphrey** crafted over 250 individual stamps to create the iconic, retro look of *The Old Truck*. The book was inspired by the strong female figures in their lives and their rural Texas landscape: "Our mom raised four sons while running the family business," they said. "Our grandmothers exuded grit and determination. Our great-grandmother bought her own farm in Louisiana with the money she'd earned picking cotton. Then, there's the common sight in Texas of old trucks set out to pasture, long forgotten and overgrown. That got us thinking about what they might have seen in all that time."

Jarrett is an author/illustrator and the former CEO of a tech startup. Jerome is an author/illustrator and a graphic designer at The Walt Disney Company. Originally from Houston, the brothers both now live in Austin, Texas.